SQUID SQUAD

Matthew Welton's poems take a playful approach to language and often blur the boundaries between poetry and other forms, such as fiction, music and visual art.

His three previous Carcanet books are: *The Book of Matthew* (2003), *We needed coffee but we'd got ourselves convinced that the later we left it the better it would taste, and, as the country grew flatter and the roads became quiet and dusk began to colour the sky, you could guess from the way we retuned the radio or unfolded the map and commented on the view that the tang of determination had overtaken our thoughts, and when, fidgety and untalkative but almost home, we drew up outside the all-night restaurant, it felt like we might just stay in the car, listening to the engine and the gentle sound of the wind* (2009) and *The Number Poems* (2016).

Matthew Welton was born in Nottingham, lives in Nottingham, and teaches creative writing at the University of Nottingham.

Matthew Welton

SQUID
SQUAD

A NOVEL

CARCANET

For Leah

First published in Great Britain in 2020 by
Carcanet
Alliance House, 30 Cross Street
Manchester M2 7AQ
www.carcanet.co.uk

A CIP catalogue record for this book is
available from the British Library.
ISBN 978 1 78410 935 6

Book design by Andrew Latimer
Printed in Great Britain by SRP Ltd, Exeter, Devon

The publisher acknowledges financial
assistance from Arts Council England.

Contents

PART I

SQUID SQUAD

I

Dustin Mostyn phones out for doughnuts and the doughnuts don't arrive. Lola Wheeler unbandages her hands. The line of spilled paint leads to Bradley Ridley's apartment.

Our shadows shift like schedules, mutters Nerys Harris as she's cycling through the subway. Lola Wheeler feeds the chaffinches the chutney. Dustin Mostyn misplaces his magnetic spoon.

A spherical lemon rolls into the kitchen. Audrey Chaudri ditches the idea that between the provable and the probable and the improvable and the improbable the parallels might be anything but inexact.

Ruth Reith snaps her catapult elastic. Audrey Chaudri kicks off her sneakers. Our hunches hatch like hornets' eggs, whispers Hank Strunk into the dictaphone. The coffee cools slowly in the blue enamel pan.

Lola Wheeler's examination of her idea of ideas brings about a shift in her definition of definition. Hank Strunk feeds the sparrows the asparagus. Natalie Chatterley's noodle ladle rusts.

Nerys Harris patches her pyjamas. Hank Strunk's cello strings snap. Angus Mingus mimes the action of rocking a baby. Lola Wheeler mutes her bassoon.

Natalie Chatterley's hunches seem reluctant to fit the structures the intellect concocts to articulate the particularity of particular things. My nerves are as numb as lemons, mumbles Nerys Harris as she's pouring away the milk.

Angus Mingus feeds the pheasants the figs. The cans of cannellini beans rust on the shelves. Hank Strunk's photograph fades. Lola Wheeler unhitches the hammock, and bundles it into her rucksack.

During the power cut Natalie Chatterley doesn't budge from behind the drum kit. Nerys Harris spits out her whisky. Bubblegum loosens Hank Strunk's teeth.

Daylight deepens like a familiar dilemma, murmurs Nerys Harris as she cycles beneath the footbridge. Kite strings tangle in the telegraph wires. Angus Mingus's mattress sags.

Where the indistinctions between things are at their most explicit, ponders Dustin Mostyn over mushroom cannelloni, the indistinctions between indistinctions may be at their most obscure.

Bradley Ridley lobs pebbles at the library windows. Squirrels squabble. The rhododendron rots. Audrey Chaudri's dictionary goes missing. Ruth Reith splits her lip on the elevator door.

Her hands are still inky as Lola Wheeler skins the small lemons and swats away the gnats. Natalie Chatterley's drumsticks go missing from her rucksack. Coffee boils slowly in the aluminium pan.

The thing about resemblances, says Natalie Chatterley, crumbling a dumpling, is that though the resemblances between resemblances are often undetectable, the resemblances between objects are seldom unclear.

Audrey Chaudri's teeth grind down. A magpie mutes its trumpet-trills. Natalie Chatterley snaps her chopsticks. The dust mites doze in the stationery drawer.

Reticence comes like a rumble of rainclouds, says Dustin Mostyn, climbing the stairs. Audrey Chaudri mimes the action of buttering toast. The lime seeds Natalie Chatterley sows sprout overnight.

#5

Nerys Harris fills a milk bottle with beer
and brings it to the bring-and-share picnic.
Bubblegum bursts on Angus Mingus's face.
Sneakers dangle from a telegraph wire.

The wind makes a sound like a curious mind,
notes Nerys Harris in her exercise book.
People point pencils at Angus Mingus.
Angus Mingus casts a fuzzy shadow.

Nerys Harris releases her balloon. A paper
boat crosses the circular pond. The fizz goes
out of Angus Mingus's cola. Nerys Harris
crumbles a stick of blue chalk.

As the batteries in the radio weaken, the songs
it plays become melancholic. Thunderclouds
thicken like thought, thinks Angus Mingus.
Nerys Harris's bicycle will rust in the rain.

Ruth Reith photographs the plump blue pigeons in the symmetrical branches of the symmetrical trees. Dustin Mostyn digs for slugs. Antiseptic does nothing for Angus Mingus's grazes.

Lola Wheeler loses at ludo. The wagtails drag their twigs through the kitchen. Audrey Chaudri breaks the intercom. Natalie Chatterley releases the wrens.

The hornets hum in harmony. Ruth Reith kicks over a stool. Lola Wheeler salts her walnuts. Someone must have borrowed Dustin Mostyn's keys.

Natalie Chatterley's mittens unravel. Small round sweet bright lemons fill the fridge. Paraffin evaporates. Audrey Chaudri swallows a tooth. There are midges in the mattress where Angus Mingus sleeps.

Natalie Chatterley pulls a page from the dictionary and hides it in the pocket of her hessian dress. Nerys Harris fast-forwards through the slow songs. The hazelnuts do nothing for Audrey Chaudri's hunger.

The gnats numb their mouths on the mulberry pulp. Audrey Chaudri's hammock hangs low. The breezes waver like whims, thinks Natalie Chatterley. Nerys Harris mimes the action of dialing a number.

Our conversations, notes Natalie Chatterley, cohere around the contention that our contentions cohere into conversations it isn't unlikely we wouldn't repeat. Daisies grow in the grit bin. The moonlight lulls.

Melon pollen gets into Audrey Chaudri's eyes. The soap won't wash out of Natalie Chatterley's sweatshirt. The gnats nest in the noodle jar. Nerys Harris's rubber boots rot.

8

Hank Strunk sucks on a block of salt. Audrey Chaudri's hands cast disproportionate shadows. Logic loosens like elastic, supposes Bradley Ridley. Ruth Reith tapes over the syncopated songs.

The things around us, notes Nerys Harris, are never exactly consistent but are inconsistent so inconsistently that their inconsistency may appear consistent.

Hank Strunk's shadow shudders. The gnats gnaw through the kettle flex. Our determination dulls like midwinter daylight, says Audrey Chaudri. Ruth Reith mashes her last potato.

Nerys Harris is still talking as the tape runs out. The lemon smell eliminates the smell of burning paper. Bradley Ridley mimes the action of popping a cork. The heavy bees blunder around in the dusk.

Angus Mingus mimes the action of reeling in a fish. Ruth Reith spits out a tooth. As she comes through the cornfield Nerys Harris calculates how far she'll have cycled by suppertime.

The crows beat Dustin Mostyn to the crumpets. Lola Wheeler wears the hems of her denims unrolled. The fireflies appear like a giddiness in the guts, says Ruth Reith. Angus Mingus's beans need stirring.

Dustin Mostyn is reluctant to reflect on what it is that is actual about the actual buzzards gathering around him in the actual pinewoods in the actual dusk. Ruth Reith makes sketches of the low sudsy clouds.

The sunlight settles like sadness, says Angus Mingus. Dustin Mostyn detunes the guitar. Ruth Reith shivers in the shower. The heavy lemons hang beyond Lola Wheeler's reach.

Natalie Chatterley uncrumples her cash.
Bradley Ridley runs a twig along the
railings. Hank Strunk scrapes up the apricot
jam. Audrey Chaudri's hiccups keep the
nuthatches awake.

Bradley Ridley's bluebells wilt. The radio
replays its rumbly tunes. Hank Strunk
imagines the fish in the fishbowl is
rethinking the distinction between objects
and objectives.

Our conversations swerve like diffident
swifts, says Natalie Chatterley as she
unlatches the gate. Angus Mingus's mattress
deflates. Audrey Chaudri mimes the action
of windscreen wipers.

Natalie Chatterley photographs the vaguely
blue finches gathering in the guttering in
the vaguely blue dusk. The letterbox flutters.
The waffle dough thaws. Nerys Harris cycles
home on punctured tyres.

Bradley Ridley restarts the stopwatch and scribbles out the numbers in his exercise book. Lola Wheeler dismantles the doorbell. Dustin Mostyn's matches don't strike.

Natalie Chatterley tramples over the marigolds. The poster peels away from the kitchen wall. Ruth Reith's theory of theory grows ostensibly indistinguishable from her theory of thought.

Angus Mingus dozes in the photo booth. Bradley Ridley's yo-yo string snaps. The reheated risotto gives Lola Wheeler bad guts. A heavy mist muffles Dustin Mostyn's trombone.

The dust mites grow resistant to the domestic disinfectant. Natalie Chatterley loses at leapfrog. Reason rubs away like rust, says Ruth Reith. Angus Mingus empties the fishbowl into the bath.

A frisbee floats in through Ruth Reith's window. Audrey Chaudri's treacle jar leaks. People point popguns at Dustin Mostyn. A tetchy swallow swelters in the apartment upstairs.

Dustin Mostyn mimes the action of sawing a log. Audrey Chaudri's harmonica rusts. The voices on the tape describe the properties of lemons. Vinegar gets into Ruth Reith's grazes.

The eloquence of melody outweighs the melody of eloquence, murmurs Dustin Mostyn as he measures out the milk. Audrey Chaudri skips over the tripwire. The wasps come like whims, says Ruth Reith.

As the wind builds, the clouds will rumble together and drift like a mild dread through the warm afternoon, Dustin Mostyn says. A blackbird twirls a twig in its mouth. Ruth Reith uncrumples her paper hat.

13

In her leaky sneakers, Natalie Chatterley drags home her bag of unripe limes. Pencil shavings blow across Ruth Reith's desk. Nerys Harris makes recordings of the doorbell.

The slump in the temperature hushes the hornets. Natalie Chatterley unbuttons her cuffs. The flowerbeds flood. The gooseberries wither. As she reads, Natalie Chatterley traces a finger along the page.

As the remit of reality relaxes, thinks Nerys Harris, the remit of rigor takes up the slack. The sparrows spit out spider bones. Summer comes, says Ruth Reith, like a riff on a rusty trumpet.

Audrey Chaudri swims into the distance. The nightingales' nervousness gets into their songs. Natalie Chatterley reheats the coffee slops. The paperclips make rust marks in Ruth Reith's notebook.

14

Audrey Chaudri glues her hands to the table. Hank Strunk winches up a bucket of rubber balls. The pauses in the pauses in the rainfall resemble the pauses in the pauses in Ruth Reith's thoughts.

The swirls of snowflakes blunt Audrey Chaudri's boredom. Ruth Reith loots the linen store. My thoughts thicken out like thistles, says Hank Strunk. Chaffinches choke on the beetle bones.

The grackles' grasp of how our idea of things determines our experience of things determines how our experience of experience will determine what it is the grackles grasp, mumbles Audrey Chaudri.

Hank Strunk slurps the salty water. The kitchen candle dwindles. Audrey Chaudri muffles her megaphone. Nerys Harris cycles through the puddle of paint.

15

Natalie Chatterley sits alone on the see-saw.
Natalie Chatterley blows into a paper bag.
The liquidized lemons ferment in a bucket.
Natalie Chatterley grinds her peanuts small.

Natalie Chatterley wrings the rain from her
sweatshirt. Natalie Chatterley's parcel paper
unrolls. Our concentration sags like satsuma
skins, says Natalie Chatterley. Small gulls
gather in the unset cement.

The focus of Natalie Chatterley's attention
drifts between the spaces between the spaces
between things and the things between the
spaces between the spaces between things.
Natalie Chatterley's sweatshirt shrinks.

The dust mites nest on the dictionary shelves.
Our thoughts flail around like fledgling
buntings, says Natalie Chatterley. The
budgerigars sulk themselves to sleep. Natalie
Chatterley's lemons don't decompose.

#16

Audrey Chaudri flings her walnuts from the window. A rubber ball rolls into a puddle of glue. Hank Strunk thinks through the increments between the infinite and the indefinite. Ruth Reith mimes the action of juggling with eggs.

Angus Mingus slurps the silty water. Hank Strunk bursts his paper bag. The radiators, thinks Audrey Chaudri, rumble like a quiet resentment. The paperclips rust in Ruth Reith's pocket.

Angus Mingus's attempts to calculate how a thing which is objectively an object might eventually become an event come practically to nothing. Ruth Reith uncrumples the paper cups.

Audrey Chaudri tugs out a tooth. A splash of lemon squash stains Angus Mingus's sweatshirt. The paperclips demagnetize. The radiators reverberate. Hank Strunk mows the moonlit lawn.

As the match burns down, Natalie Chatterley passes it between the fingers of her right hand and the fingers of her left. The can of cocoa beans corrodes. Angus Mingus's pillow splits open.

Ruth Reith unstitches the patches from her denims. Bradley Ridley mimes the action of trimming his nails. Desire dissolves like salt, murmurs Lola Wheeler. Dustin Mostyn's doughnut dough won't thaw.

The erosion of the process of erosion is cut short by the process of the erosion of process, thinks Ruth Reith. Bradley Ridley ties his shoes in an ununravellable knot

Nerys Harris draws zigzags on the dusty table. The radio resumes its woozy songs. Natalie Chatterley returns the robin to the rusty cage. A line of paper windmills rotate on the lawn.

#18

Lola Wheeler takes down the mirror and gazes at the wall. The pebbles wear holes in Audrey Chaudri's pockets. Hank Strunk detaches the balloon string from its rectangle of card.

Lola Wheeler recites from the reference books on the relation between the relations between the relations between things. Audrey Chaudri's matches are too damp to strike.

Hank Strunk uncrumples the typewriter paper. The herons hover in on an intermittent wind. Lola Wheeler snaps her hacksaw blade. Rainwater runs off the corrugated roof.

Hank Strunk feeds the larks the lawn seed. Audrey Chaudri lets her wristwatch wind down. The shallow river ripples like a slow realisation, says Lola Wheeler over a glitchy phone line.

Angus Mingus catapults pebbles at the lemonade cans on the wall. Natalie Chatterley appears in the photograph twice. The salty spaghetti gives Hank Strunk rumbly guts.

The raffia unravels in Nerys Harris's hands. A blue crow chews through the crocus roots. Angus Mingus pours coffee into an ice-cube tray and places it in the freezer.

As her concentration curdles, Nerys Harris suggests that in theory the theory that theory requires practical proof probably requires little practical proof.

Angus Mingus returns to the library and draws doodles in the dictionary. The midges grow like grudges, Nerys Harris says. Angus Mingus slits open his mattress. Hank Strunk's rubber boots rot in the rain.

Audrey Chaudri draws around her left hand, then sharpens her pencil and draws around her right. Nerys Harris's cider sours. As it bounces, Bradley Ridley's wet tennis ball leaves its outline across the pavement.

Natalie Chatterley muffles her timpani drums. The moths get lost in the rigorous mist. Sassiness softens like sandpaper, says Ruth Reith and stretches out on the bench.

Hank Strunk mimes the action of unpeeling a banana. Thistles rustle in the fitful wind. Our conversations convey little besides the conventions of conversation, Lola Wheeler supposes out loud.

Ruth Reith walks out of the walk-in refrigerator. Angus Mingus shivers in his towel. Nuthatches nest in Nerys Harris's bike basket. Lola Wheeler skulks home in her socks.

Dustin Mostyn weights the balloon string with paperclips and watches for it to come to rest in mid-air. Bradley Ridley mimes the action of flipping a coin. The scrawny herons urinate in Ruth Reith's hedge.

Dustin Mostyn holds the envelope above the steaming kettle. Natalie Chatterley's snapdragons droop. As she climbs through the railings, Ruth Reith snags her sweatshirt. Bradley Ridley's spinach boils dry.

Bradley Ridley rips up the flip-chart paper. A slug slides up the kitchen wall. Ruth Reith retracts her retraction that only reluctance comes only reluctantly.

The pencil pokes a hole in Dustin Mostyn's pocket. A small crow croaks its croony tune. Reason rattles like a rusty bike, says Nerys Harris, tossing a spatula between her hands.

As the temperature jumps and the loop of tape warps, the uncertainty goes out of Lola Wheeler's voice. The felt-tips leak into Angus Mingus's pocket. Audrey Chaudri detunes her ukulele.

In midwinter the daylight deepens like doubt, says Natalie Chatterley. Nerys Harris's beach ball bounces into the brambles. The tulips droop as Audrey Chaudri walks by.

When the principle of pragmatism makes way for the pragmatism of principle, says Dustin Mostyn, it happens on a hunch. Audrey Chaudri's sawblade rusts.

The lentils leak out of Audrey Chaudri's homemade maracas. The woodpeckers reckon on the willow trees' resilience. Where the shallow river narrows, Lola Wheeler paddles home.

Ruth Reith locks the apartment and posts back the key through the letterbox. Dustin Mostyn loosens his lute strings. Natalie Chatterley makes notations of the gnats' flustery flight.

Rain comes like a resumption in the rigor of things, Nerys Harris says, and grips her pencil between her teeth. The lemon tree trembles. Dustin Mostyn dozes in the thistly grass.

In practice the theory that practice requires a theoretical basis requires very little theoretical basis, says Natalie Chatterley in her letter. Ruth Reith mimes the action of ringing a church bell.

Nerys Harris lets the beetle out of its matchbox. Sunlight subdues the sparrows' songs. Dustin Mostyn's gravel shovel rusts. A spiral of apple peel yellows on Ruth Reith's plate.

As we allow our idea of a thing to soften into specifics, we lose our grasp of the thing the thing actually is, Angus Mingus imagines. Natalie Chatterley sharpens each end of her pencil.

Angus Mingus pieces together the ripped-up letter. Natalie Chatterley swallows the silty beer. Angus Mingus steps onto the bathroom scales with the watermelon in his hands.

The hornets hang around like a late-morning headache, Angus Mingus says. Natalie Chatterley turns her sweatshirt inside out. Midges get into the mustard jar. Natalie Chatterley's fever cools.

Angus Mingus's new tattoo washes off. Natalie Chatterley's broom pole breaks. The gulls gawp in at the kitchen window. The pages of Angus Mingus's sketchbook scatter in the wind.

As she walks in a widening circle, Lola Wheeler leaves a spiral of footprints in the snow. Bradley Ridley feeds the chickens the chestnuts. Natalie Chatterley drums on an upturned bucket.

Any metaphor is a metaphor for the idea of metaphor, Natalie Chatterley mutters. Chaffinches chew at the chocolate sultanas. The hum of the hand drier harmonises with the hum of the electric lights.

Lola Wheeler hopscotches across the tarmac. Bradley Ridley's beach ball won't blow up. From the woodpeckers' perspective perspective means nothing, Hank Strunk says.

The midges move like smudges. Natalie Chatterley weighs out her walnuts again. Knowing knowing gets us nowhere gets us nowhere, thinks Hank Strunk. Lola Wheeler skips ahead.

As she crosses the park, Audrey Chaudri leaves a line of peanut shells behind her. A ladder leans up beneath Nerys Harris's window. Dustin Mostyn twangs his wooden ruler.

Ruth Reith sketches a brickwork pattern on the plain white kitchen wall. A raven rephrases the robin's song. The rhythms of reticence unravel like rope, Audrey Chaudri says.

The wind comes like a wallop of whimsy, says Bradley Ridley. Gnats nibble at Dustin Mostyn's limbs. The sparrows spit out the spinach seeds. Nerys Harris mimes the action of grinding pepper.

Without the thoughts we're unaware we think, thinks Ruth Reith, the thoughts we're sure we're sure of might possibly not be possible. Bradley Ridley wades upriver. A warm wind hurries the small hawks home.

Nerys Harris blows through a drinking straw into a basin of bubble bath mixture. The drizzle wrinkles Dustin Mostyn's writing paper. Mayflies get into the maple syrup.

Angus Mingus tips his chair backwards. Natalie Chatterley aims the spray can at a lighted match. Hank Strunk's beer sours. Audrey Chaudri mimes the action of pumping up a tyre.

As she wallows through the shallows, Ruth Reith imagines that between technology and technique there is technically no distinction.

Fog fades away like forgiveness, says Bradley Ridley. A grid of weeds grows through the gaps between the slabs. Natalie Chatterley's bathwater spills over. Lola Wheeler leaves the caps off her felt-tip pens.

On a breezy morning Lola Wheeler strings her hammock beneath the apple tree. Natalie Chatterley's radio retunes itself. A key hangs on a string inside Angus Mingus's letterbox.

Angus Mingus's two wristwatches run at different speeds. Natalie Chatterley unfolds her paper hat. Our woes unwind like lemon rind, whispers Lola Wheeler to herself.

As the theoretical thrum of theory fades in, the hypothetical hum of hypothesis dwindles away, Angus Mingus mutters. Lola Wheeler's pencil sharpener rusts.

Angus Mingus unpeels his peach. The woodpeckers snack on the skinny yellow slugs. Natalie Chatterley dims the strip lights. Air squeaks from the neck of Lola Wheeler's balloon.

#29

Hank Strunk places the edge of the mirror down the centre of the photograph of her face. The fuzzy clouds fade into each other. Nerys Harris's raft drifts ashore.

The radiator rattles like over-readiness, notes Nerys Harris. Hank Strunk holds a match to the frayed end of the rope. Nerys Harris mimes the action of focusing a pair of binoculars.

Nerys Harris contemplates the changes that take place when the processes everything goes through go through the processes everything goes through. Hank Strunk uncrumples the paper boat.

Hank Strunk dims the desk lamps. The finches flinch. A hummingbird hoots. In her paper trousers Nerys Harris wanders out into the intermittent rain.

Bradley Ridley falls asleep reading, and wakes with newsprint on his face. Natalie Chatterley patches the patches on her denims. Ruth Reith walks backwards into the untouched snow.

Reason rots like pears, Dustin Mostyn says. A balloon floats over the cactus patch. The clouds, says Natalie Chatterley, come like an unbudgeable kind of boredom.

We create a vernacular particular to whatever mustn't be unsaid, says Ruth Reith. Dustin Mostyn fabricates a rubric for the fabrication of rubric.

Bradley Ridley mouths along to the radio adverts. The blue crows croon their crotchety song. Ruth Reith flips another coin. Nerys Harris cycles out into the resolute rain.

On the balcony, Lola Wheeler practises her yo-yo tricks. Natalie Chatterley detunes her drums. At the narrow window Ruth Reith's narrow face appears. Angus Mingus gives the peaches a squeeze.

Hornets hover like hopefulness, Audrey Chaudri says. Doves descend like a mild delirium, says Dustin Mostyn. Ruth Reith wraps her hands in sticky-tape, sticky side out.

Angus Mingus takes down the bunting. The pheasants fade into the fog. Audrey Chaudri swivels on her chair. Lola Wheeler unpeels a ready-sliced banana.

The facts don't fit Natalie Chatterley's theory that there is no theory the facts particularly fit. Dustin Mostyn unrolls more bubble wrap. The low stars light the unweeded yard.

32

Bradley Ridley makes a mixtape of songs that can be sung in a single breath. Natalie Chatterley mimes the action of paddling a canoe. In the dusty mirror Hank Strunk draws matchstick people.

A robin gets in through the kitchen window and sits like a self at the centre of things, Lola Wheeler says. Damp gets into the sugar shaker. Bradley Ridley mimes the action of drinking through a straw.

The form formlessness takes, thinks Lola Wheeler, informs the form form will take in its absence. The ravens return like a rigorous form of reluctance, Bradley Ridley admits.

In the sheet of card, Hank Strunk cuts out the stencil of a star. Natalie Chatterley patches the patches on the patches on her sweatshirt. In the lemon tree the wrens rehearse their solemn song.

#33

Angus Mingus sticks a pin into the inflatable globe. Lola Wheeler mists up the mirror with her breath. The grit won't wash out of Ruth Reith's grazes. Bradley Ridley's thesaurus thuds shut.

Drawing-pin divots pattern the unpainted wall. The bubbleless beer gives Bradley Ridley the burps. Nerys Harris dissembles her rickety bike. Angus Mingus mimes the action of striking a match.

The peregrines' inherently intelligent demeanor hinders their indifference to the thinkiness of thought, mumbles Lola Wheeler as she's unbolting the gate.

Nerys Harris squeezes glue into the padlock. Lola Wheeler's umbrella stem snaps. Peanut peelings blow out into the yard. Angus Mingus draws squiggles on the unswept floor.

34

Audrey Chaudri drags a magnet through the little heap of paperclips. Somebody seems to have sewn up Dustin Mostyn's trouser pockets. Natalie Chatterley sucks on a block of frozen beer.

Audrey Chaudri mimes the action of tightening a screw. Things discontinue continually, says Natalie Chatterley. Dustin Mostyn topples the stack of books. Vinegar trickles into the sink.

Dustin Mostyn's key snaps off in the lock. The towel rails rust. Do midges begrudge us our malleable memories? wonders Audrey Chaudri as she's peppering her soup.

The candles in Natalie Chatterley's windows flicker. The pelicans' pangs for pecans resume. Audrey Chaudri snaps her mop in two. The tide washes Dustin Mostyn's footprints away.

35

Angus Mingus's alarm clock totters off the bedside table. Nerys Harris re-dilutes her blueberry juice. A desk fan swivels in Angus Mingus's window. The pile of polyester dusters depletes.

Nerys Harris holds the loudest notes the longest. Angus Mingus photographs the reflection of his reflection. The low stars linger like laziness, sings Angus Mingus. Nerys Harris's picnic blanket frays.

Nerys Harris's narrow face appears at the narrow window. The towel rail won't dry Angus Mingus's pyjamas. Nerys Harris writes with a pencil in each hand.

Somebody seems to have removed the pea from Angus Mingus's whistle. A pigeon flies in through the upstairs window, and out through the window downstairs.

#36

Nerys Harris curls a strip of paper against the blade of the kitchen scissors. Lola Wheeler smudges the ink stamp on the back of her hand.

Hank Strunk's key fits none of the locks. Ruth Reith hides her camera in the eiderdown cupboard. A paper boat drifts towards the deep end of the pool.

Credibility creaks like an uncreosoted fence, Angus Mingus mumbles. Dustin Mostyn pleats the pages of the letter. The out-of-focus photographs scatter in the wind.

Natalie Chatterley takes her foot off the garden hose. Bradley Ridley's bubblegum loses its stretch. A flamingo flutters its weary wings. Audrey Chaudri walks home on her hands.

37

Natalie Chatterley holds two telephones together, mouthpiece to earpiece, earpiece to mouthpiece. Ruth Reith shades in the zeros on each page of the magazine.

Angus Mingus topples a stack of pebbles. Someone's cut the buttons off Hank Strunk's shirt. The rhododendrons rehydrate. Natalie Chatterley can't find herself in the photograph.

The low clouds cluster like minor calamities, mumbles Ruth Reith as she's arriving at the rehearsal. Angus Mingus lets the rice boil dry.

The daffodils stiffen in the starchy soil. The streetlights flutter. The swifts' wings wilt. Hank Strunk slams on the brakes.

Lola Wheeler mimes the action of focusing a telescope. The missing street-map reappears on Nerys Harris's wall. The tyre swing sways in the drizzle. Bradley Ridley folds the photocopy inky-side out.

Bradley Ridley wades out into the lake. The short bananas ripen fast. If someone will bring the chess figures, Nerys Harris will bring the board.

Gas jets hiss like the persistence of persistence, thinks Lola Wheeler as she's hanging from the monkey bars. The small swans swallow the swollen limes. Bradley Ridley's jam jar dangles in the stream.

Lola Wheeler fans out the photographs. Damp gets into the sugar shaker. Nerys Harris pockets a scrabble tile. The fritter batter bubbles in the shallow blue jug.

#39

Hank Strunk squirts detergent into the city-centre fountain. Audrey Chaudri mimes the action of swimming the crawl. As Ruth Reith unlocks the back door, the front door blows shut.

The bleachy smell stifles the smell of warm waffles. Angus Mingus's cello is missing a string. Hank Strunk releases the bees from the marmalade jar.

Does the way our minds magnify our moods cause our moods to magnify our minds? Ruth Reith wonders. Audrey Chaudri cuts a notch in the doorpost just above the height of her head.

Angus Mingus's pillow deflates. The apples soften. The onions splutter. The riffs the ravens return to repeat in Hank Strunk's mind.

#40

Nerys Harris retrieves her rusty bike from the rusty bicycle rack. Dustin Mostyn trips over the skipping rope. Our moods flatten like flute-notes, Natalie Chatterley admits.

The smell of winter dill dilutes the smell of disinfectant. Lola Wheeler licks up the lemon juice. Somebody's left their teeth marks in Natalie Chatterley's pencil.

Rigor unravels like rope, thinks Nerys Harris. Dustin Mostyn spreads the photos facedown on the floor. Lola Wheeler erases the asterisks from the margins of her book.

Nerys Harris licks her salty fingers. Dustin Mostyn's ladder is missing a rung. The raucous storks rephrase their squawks. Lola Wheeler swims ashore.

Natalie Chatterley tramples a path through the fields behind the apartment. Ruth Reith imitates the action of flipping a pancake. Somebody seems to have drained the liquid from Audrey Chaudri's spirit level.

Audrey Chaudri empties the biscuit basket. The ginger beer cools Ruth Reith's fever. The midsummer breezes scatter the gnats. Natalie Chatterley draws around the rim of the upturned jar.

The imperative narrative gives us disguises the inconsequentiality inherent in things, thinks Audrey Chaudri as she's skinning a plum.

The gooseberries give Ruth Reith fluttery guts. The fritter batter won't defrost. Where the river runs deepest, notices Natalie Chatterley, the fish swim slow.

#42

Nerys Harris pinches out her birthday candles. Dustin Mostyn's wristwatch rusts. Someone's removed the clapper from Bradley Ridley's bell. The rungs of the wooden ladder rot in the rain.

As Natalie Chatterley tugs the rope towards her, the bucket edges further away. The melon seeds swell in the swallows' guts. Doubt deepens like a sleepy river, Nerys Harris supposes.

Dustin Mostyn mimes the action of knocking at a door. Wistfulness wears down, thinks Lola Wheeler, like the workings of the wind.

Bradley Ridley's mittens shrink in the drizzle. A beetle scuttles between the bricks. On the tree in Lola Wheeler's yard, luminescent lemons appear.

#43

Angus Mingus memorises the map and wanders out into the village. A rope swing dangles from a brittle branch. Ruth Reith reassembles the extractor fan.

Natalie Chatterley places a hanky over the mouthpiece of the phone. Soap bubbles blow out through the kitchen window. The river trickles away like tranquility or trust, Ruth Reith says.

The recording of a vulture's screeches repeats on the kitchen radio. Beans burble on the stove. Angus Mingus draws smileys in the sand.

The radishes make the robins retch. As she dismantles the ladders, Natalie Chatterley considers whether the spring winds flurry like worthiness or worry.

#44

Hank Strunk pockets a piece of the jigsaw. Lola Wheeler rolls herself up in the rug. The wagtails worry they worry too little. The trap door flips open and out jumps Audrey Chaudri.

As she rewinds the rehearsal tape, Audrey Chaudri considers whether, while our doubts dispel our determination, our determination affects our doubts at all.

Hank Strunk spits out the ping-pong balls. Lola Wheeler holds a phone to each ear. Audrey Chaudri prints out her photograph back-to-front. The wheatears give another whoop.

Hank Strunk mimes the action of a beginner violinist. The fog fizzles away. The gulls tug at the lugworms and the lugworms tug back. Lola Wheeler counts her footsteps out loud.

#45

Angus Mingus squirts out a squiggle of mustard. Angus Mingus rolls his watermelons home. Somebody has cut eyeholes in Angus Mingus's bedsheets. The walnut sapling wilts in the drought.

Angus Mingus tips out the sand from his sneakers. The toucans' pangs for pecans decrease. Angus Mingus's raft drifts upriver. The cool soil curtails the cactuses' growth.

Angus Mingus miscalculates how he miscalculates how he miscalculates. The weary canaries witter all night. Angus Mingus folds down the corner of every page in the book.

Angus Mingus finds the matchbox is full of spent matches. Chaffinches chunter. A beach ball bursts. Angus Mingus licks up the whisky. Angus Mingus's key snaps off in the lock.

#46

Nerys Harris rings every bell in the bike shed. Lola Wheeler mimes the action of combing her hair. Ravens root around in the rhubarb patch. Bradley Ridley's typewriter rusts.

As the timpani symphony replays on the radio, Natalie Chatterley wonders whether existence isn't an inexertive form of thought. A slug slides over the kitchen floor.

The pinecones unclench on Nerys Harris's window ledge. The chickens don't reckon the rain will ease let up. Lola Wheeler turns her pockets inside out.

Bradley Ridley scatters his walnuts. The lemon-wood logs burn away fast. Natalie Chatterley makes transcriptions of the grebes' gruff tune.

#47

Angus Mingus glues the lid onto the marmalade jar. Bradley Ridley untangles a bundle of yarn. The breezes ruffle the puffin down. Ruth Reith's window blinds are missing a slat.

Determination droops like a birthday balloon, says Bradley Ridley in a letter. The mists resist the rigorous wind. Until the toucan's spoken, Ruth Reith says, the blue jays are saying nothing.

Each coin Bradley Ridley flips lands tails up. Angus Mingus jangles his keys. The thought of order interrupts the order of Ruth Reith's thoughts.

Bradley Ridley's candles never stay lit. A paper boat floats in the aluminium bath. Reality rolls on like something under-rehearsed, says Ruth Reith to herself.

#48

As she's sketching, Audrey Chaudri's pencil never lifts from the page. The daisies in Lola Wheeler's jam jar wilt. Dustin Mostyn feeds the beetles the beetroot seeds.

Nettle stems tremble like trust, thinks Audrey Chaudri. The chaffinches choke on the chilli-pepper chowder. Ruth Reith uncrumples the typing paper. Lola Wheeler bites into a block of blue soap.

The limits we impose on the language precipitate the limits the language imposes on us, Dustin Mostyn sings to himself.

Ruth Reith unfolds her paper hat. The gannets repeat the linnets' song. Lola Wheeler walks backwards from the beach until she can hear the waves no longer.

#49

Natalie Chatterley bundles her socks into unmatching pairs. The jam oozes out of Dustin Mostyn's doughnut. Ruth Reith blunts every knife in the drawer.

Natalie Chatterley mimes the action of swimming the backstroke. Angus Mingus's lilo deflates. Thoughts branch out from thoughts at a stringent tangent, thinks Dustin Mostyn out loud.

Ruth Reith lets an ice cube melt in her hand. The pelican's skeleton shrinks in the winter. Natalie Chatterley unfolds her paper boat.

As she sits in the thistles, Ruth Reith suggests that language is what we're left with when we're through with communication. Angus Mingus's skipping rope frays.

The starchy earth stifles the sunflowers'
growth. A rake floats in the swimming pool.
Herons hatch. Wagtails wince. Rain smudges
Bradley Ridley's handwritten map.

Flute notes flutter like secret feelings, thinks
Lola Wheeler as she crumples up the tickets.
Natalie Chatterley splits the drum skin.
Bradley Ridley's jigsaw is missing a piece.

The low winds weaken like whimsicality or
want, thinks Hank Strunk as the bathwater
empties. Bicycles rust. Rhubarb rots. Lola
Wheeler kicks open a door.

Natalie Chatterley twangs her wooden ruler.
Swallows swirl in on a spiral of breeze. Hank
Strunk refills the cartridge of his ink pen
with water. Natalie Chatterley wades ashore.

As Lola Wheeler catches the lime in her right hand, she lets go of the lemon in her left. Angus Mingus lights a candle from a dying candle.

Difference comes down to specifics, thinks Lola Wheeler, as much as specifics come down to difference. The rooks peck at the rye seeds. Angus Mingus leaves the key in the lock.

Lola Wheeler hooks a paperclip to a paperclip. Angus Mingus feeds the egrets the yeasty toast. The strip of sticky tape rips away from Lola Wheeler's forearm.

Does the mind, wonders Angus Mingus, make any distinction between the melting point of memory and the freezing point of mood? The beer bottles cool in the aluminium sink.

Natalie Chatterley stirs her coffee with the blunt end of a drumstick. The finches flinch. The ice cream melts. Natalie Chatterley hides her hands in her sweatshirt sleeves.

Natalie Chatterley's balloon floats to the ceiling. The dry rice softens in Natalie Chatterley's mouth. The rhythm of rhetoric regulates the rhetoric of rhythm, says Natalie Chatterley, and sighs.

Natalie Chatterley studies her reflection in the drizzly upstairs window. The wasps' mood wavers. The afternoon lengthens. Natalie Chatterley mimes the action of taking a picture.

The dimension of our ideas dictates our idea of dimension, sings Natalie Chatterley to herself. On the hook behind the kitchen door hang Natalie Chatterley's headphones.

#53

Audrey Chaudri re-corks the bottle and lobs it from the end of the pier. Nerys Harris removes the thumbtacks from the soles of her sneakers.

The pan of onions splutters like a lengthy explanation, says Lola Wheeler, and shrugs. Audrey Chaudri draws spirals in the unwashed windows. Nerys Harris shuffles her index cards.

Do the causes of causes counterbalance the effects of effects? thinks Lola Wheeler. The gulls' trills sharpen. The doughnut dough thaws.

Audrey Chaudri presses hard with her pencil. A blue fog fills the laundry room. Lola Wheeler lobs her lemons from one bank of the canal to the other.

#54

Natalie Chatterley fills her water pistol with vinegar. Lola Wheeler squeezes lemon into her grazes. As the beetles scuttle beneath them, the yellow nettles wilt.

Reality rolls in like something unrehearsed, says Hank Strunk into the telephone. Dustin Mostyn blunts all the pencils in the pencil tin.

Do our hunches hinder our understanding, wonders Natalie Chatterley, or does our understanding hinder our hunches? The small crows cringe. Clouds scuff through the skies.

Lola Wheeler spits on her fingers. Hank Strunk mimes the action of shuffling cards. The tadpoles escape from the jam jar. Dustin Mostyn lifts the doormat and finds no key.

The tides wash away the squiggles Bradley Ridley scrawls in the sand. Ruth Reith flattens out her origami helter-skelter and reassembles it as an octopus.

Lola Wheeler slices a lemon lengthwise. The robins regurgitate the under-ripe raspberries. Things go through phases of going through phases, Bradley Ridley mumbles.

Ruth Reith mimes the action of blowing up a balloon. Rainwater pools on Lola Wheeler's roof. Fog fizzles out like a shallow fascination, says Bradley Ridley between sneezes.

Ruth Reith unfolds her paper boat. A sparrow's shadow crosses the wall. The mind misaligns with the waning moon, says Lola Wheeler and unbuttons her cuffs.

#56

Audrey Chaudri's popcorn won't pop. Nerys Harris draws smileys in the misted glass. Somebody's been pouring peanuts through Angus Mingus's letterbox.

Determination deepens like a dull summer cloud, says Audrey Chaudri between burps. Nerys Harris shelves her books with the spines facing inwards.

Sparrows perch on the handlebars of Nerys Harris's bike. Angus Mingus turns the street map the other way up. The mist thins away like a mild intrigue, says Audrey Chaudri to herself.

Nerys Harris films herself filming herself. Angus Mingus tilts the table. The squirrels beat the sparrows to the birdseed in Audrey Chaudri's yard.

#57

Natalie Chatterley flattens her face against the window. The rain washes away the hopscotch grid. Dustin Mostyn sows a spiral of fast-growing sunflowers.

Definitions stiffen like late-summer winds, says Natalie Chatterley between hiccups. Dustin Mostyn mimes the action of threading a needle. Natalie Chatterley's kettle boils dry.

The crunch goes out of Dustin Mostyn's onions. Natalie Chatterley files down the teeth of her keys. A wooden stool topples. Candlewax pools on Dustin Mostyn's desk.

Dread drags in like early winter drizzle, thinks Natalie Chatterley. Crows' bones creak. Fish dash downstream. Dustin Mostyn climbs along the branch and unties the rope swing.

#58

With each step Ruth Reith shortens her stride. Audrey Chaudri's bananas bruise. The tarmac softens. The phone wire frays. Hank Strunk sings along with the speeded-up tape.

The thoroughness of the thought of thoroughness underlies the thought of the thoroughness of thought, thinks Ruth Reith.

In the yard the logs rot. Audrey Chaudri sips from the river. In the fridge the celery yellows. Ruth Reith unwraps the cling film from her hands.

The clouds go by like something no one's saying, writes Audrey Chaudri in her diary. Hank Strunk draws squiggles in the fresh cement. As the sun's beginning rising the ravens leave the roof.

59

Angus Mingus releases the hornets from the jam jar. The key slips off the string around Bradley Ridley's neck. Natalie Chatterley returns the matches to the matchbox.

Natalie Chatterley mimes the action of swimming the breaststroke. The laces of Angus Mingus's sneakers fray. Bradley Ridley draws round the rim of an upturned coffee cup.

The idea of particularity, thinks Natalie Chatterley, inhibits the particularity of ideas. The narrow stream quickens. The wagtails wake in a fitful wind.

Autumn comes like something someone's mumbling, says Angus Mingus. Bradley Ridley's handprints won't wash off the windows. Natalie Chatterley's rubber ball loses its bounce.

#60

Ruth Reith's pogo stick leaves dimples in the lawn. Nerys Harris feeds the chickens the chilli seeds. Hank Strunk mimes the action of a pneumatic drill.

My moods meander like a thin winter mist, Nerys Harris says. The flamingoes' pangs for pecans weaken. Ruth Reith mashes raspberries between her hands.

There is no world external to the thought of an external world, says Nerys Harris as she's hurrying her lunch. Hawklings hover like high notes. Fog bundles in.

Hank Strunk's kettle flex frays. The egg timer empties. The slower gnats scatter. The line of Ruth Reith's footprints dissects the dewy meadow.

Lola Wheeler flattens out her origami windmill and reassembles it as a giraffe. The sunlight fades like fascination, says Bradley Ridley, and gulps.

On the tape of the discussion of the tape of the discussion, Audrey Chaudri scarcely sounds like herself. The rain resumes its unscriptable rhythm.

Winter comes like something you wouldn't say out loud, says Lola Wheeler into the phone. Bradley Ridley removes a pebble from the pile.

Audrey Chaudri throws the crows the samosas. The zip on Lola Wheeler's anorak snags. In a sheet of stiff card, Bradley Ridley cuts out the stencil of a smiley.

Natalie Chatterley rips up the map and ambles out into the snow. The elastic in Dustin Mostyn's swimming goggles slacken. Bradley Ridley's paper boat sails across the puddle.

The currents of the a heron's thoughts correspond with the currents of the wind, Ruth Reith says. Audrey Chaudri folds her anorak into the pocket of her anorak.

The mind manufactures its melodies no more than the melodies manufacture the mind, Angus Mingus thinks out loud. The abrupter breezes rile the rooks.

Our moods drift like a drowsy cloud, Hank Strunk says. A pile of pennies topples. Nerys Harris imitates the action of playing the concertina.

Lola Wheeler strikes a match and, as it burns, begins counting. Angus Mingus wedges the window shut. The key on the string round Nerys Harris's neck doesn't fit her door.

The spring wind cools like confidence, thinks Natalie Chatterley. The goose's guts rumble. The shallow clouds shift. Lola Wheeler holds a match to the frayed end of the rope.

On the wet sand Nerys Harris cycles in a spiral. Angus Mingus taps on the heat pipes. The deep river slows. Somebody's taken the laces from Natalie Chatterley's sneakers.

Moths chew at the mop head. Lola Wheeler loosens a screw. We deal with difficulty with difficulty, Natalie Chatterley says. Angus Mingus tips forward on his chair.

#64

Natalie Chatterley butters each side of her bread. Hank Strunk mimes the action of flipping a coin. Dustin Mostyn pokes a finger into the mousetrap. Somebody's sawn up Ruth Reith's stilts.

Indiscipline dies away like a low winter wind, thinks Natalie Chatterley and shoulders open the door. The gulls' pulse quickens. Hank Strunk mows the mulchy meadow.

Ruth Reith sings the lowest notes the loudest. Dustin Mostyn dabs his thumb into the salt. We need to nullify our need to nullify our needs, Hank Strunk mumbles as he's unrolling the rug.

Dustin Mostyn glues the plug into the socket. Natalie Chatterley unpicks the grass-seed darts from her sweater. Ruth Reith dismantles her matchstick giraffe and reconstructs it as a windmill.

PART II

How long could we live off peanuts and pickles?
What about whisky? Whose photograph's that?
What's the word for what it means to feel no doubt
you feel no doubt? Will you sell me your pencil?
How deep is the mist?

How would I know if you were taping our
conversations? What's in the water? Who was in
the hammock? Is the radio okay or is it just the
signal? Why buy a ticket if you're not taking the
train?

What about the wasps? Did you wind your watch
this morning? Is anybody going to finish this
soup? What will we do if, with no movement
from us, the shadows of our hands make gestures
of their own?

What's in the jam jar? Whose sneakers are those?
Didn't you send the postcards until you'd come
home? Shouldn't we leave a note to say which road
we'll be taking? Is the tape still running? Is this
bridge on the map?

What if the breadth of our definitions doesn't
depend on our definition of breadth? Who wants
a lemon? How easily do you bruise? What is there
to stop me rejigging your words to make them say
something you might not mean?

How old's your toothbrush? Where'd you put the paracetamol? Won't you be feeding the fishes? Does meaning make up for the absence of melody? When is a reason not a reason? Isn't there more chocolate?

Where did you learn to punch that hard? Where did you leave the suitcase? Could you sell me a stamp? Can nothing stop us thinking nothing can stop us thinking? What good's a good voice if your tunes are bad?

What if the camera jams? Isn't there more vinegar? Which were the pages you ripped from the book? Isn't there another way out of the kitchen? Is whimsy worse than wordlessness? What's holding us back?

POEM FOR SARAH JACKSON

a phone call
to a village

where the lemons
are yet

to ripen
from a village

where the lemons
are already ripe

Grade	Descriptors	Exemplars
86 – 100%	Creatively green, insightfully green; illuminating, inspiring; exciting, authoritative.	Churchyard ivy, red-wine bottles, card-table baize, mature pike, cavolo nero.
70 – 85%	Persuasively green; sophisticated and original in its greenness; ambitiously, meticulously, critically green; convincingly or unexpectedly green.	Pinewoods in late summer after rain, snooker-table baize, wilted spinach, Starboard navigation lights, the bruising around a black eye after 2–3 days.
60 – 69%	Fluently and thoroughly green; precise; rigorous.	The seaweed in Norfolk, the Lyle's Golden Syrup tin, white-wine bottles, kale, the flex of the Christmas-tree lights.
50 – 59%	Clearly, confidently, consistently green; accurately green; carefully, congruently, coherently green.	Ping-pong tables, the wicket at Trent Bridge, boiled green lentils, Bramleys, the Wicked Witch of the West.
40 – 49%	Satisfactorily and sufficiently green; adequate.	The wicket at Edgbaston, Rose's Lime Marmalade, the Incredible Hulk, Granny Smiths, rock crabs, mushy peas.
35 – 39%	Incompletely, inadequately, inconsistently green; derivative or limited in its greenness; superficially green; irrelevantly green.	Broad beans, the wicket at Headingley, the green tinge of a bluebottle, dry moss, gardeners' twine.
20 – 34%	Erroneously/wrongly green; extremely limited in its greenness; inappropriate; insufficiently or incoherently green.	The grass after a short drought, budgerigars' feathers, boiled brown lentils, oxidized copper, the seaweed in Suffolk.
0- 19%	Greenness absent or lacking; formless; detrimental to greenness.	The grass where a tent has been, mint-flavour Durex, mould, the bruising around a black eye after 4–5 days, the vinegar in the jar after the pickles are finished.

Grade	Descriptors	Exemplars
86 – 100%	Insight in bringing new perspectives to bear on blueness, or in developing new knowledge of blue.	Shrink-to-fit denim, Biro ink, tarmac before it cools, peacoat wool, hedgerow blackberries in early September.
70 – 85%	An ambitious blue carried out successfully, with sophisticated handling of blueness.	The Duke of Wellington £5 note, Raspberry Slush Puppies, the dusk in late August, Guernsey fisherman's sweaters, the neutral wire in electrical cable.
60 – 69%	Highly competent in presentation of blueness; appropriate and intelligent use of blue.	The flame of mains methane, the Smurfs, Banda machine ink, nylon tarpaulins, an Oyster card.
50 – 59%	Conscientiously blue; focused and balanced with at least a reasonable understanding of blueness.	Cropwell Bishop stilton, preshrunk denim, municipal swimming pools, a peacock's feathers, the Elizabeth Fry £5 note.
40 – 49%	Accurately blue, with some elements of partial or pedestrian blueness.	Antibacterial hand-sanitiser gel, copper sulphate solution, the milkman's trousers, nylon rope, pregnancy tester kit indicator.
35 – 39%	Not more than basically blue.	Colston Bassett stilton, a kingfisher's feathers, chambray, the spark from a cigarette-lighter, a black maria's flashing light.
20 – 34%	Insufficient evidence of basic blueness; ineptly blue.	The Winston Churchill £5 note, Calor gas flames, cornershop carrier bags, human veins, the January dawn.
0- 19%	Disappointing in its grasp of blueness.	The glow of an insect electrocutor, faded denim, pool cue chalk, dental mouthwash, cigarette smoke.

Grade	Descriptors	Exemplars
86 – 100%	An exceptional demonstration of black; a synthesis of black, in both breadth and depth, beyond the prescribed range; excellent; black beyond expectation.	Cast-iron griddle pans, rooks' feathers, Guinness Extra, the insides of a telescope, the wick of a burning candle.
70 – 85%	Outstanding/excellent understanding of black; typically excellent in its demonstration and performance of black.	Burned toast, marmite, the insides of a clarinet, marble headstones, resin.
60 – 69%	Very good ability to apply blackness in an appropriate selection of contexts; demonstrates autonomy in approach though may occasionally rely on set sources of black.	Double espresso, newly inked stamp pads, liquorice bootlaces, crotchets, Pepsi-Cola.
50 – 59%	Solid approach to black though may be limited in the clarity or coherence of its blackness.	Guinness Export, vinyl LPs, mushroom gills, shading with the flat of a 9B pencil, domestic coal.
40 – 49%	Blackness is sufficient to deal with basic concepts and contexts but fails to make meaningful or adequately constructed advances over a full range of perspectives on black.	Discarded coffee grounds, school trousers, hi-fi equipment fascia, coke, wagtail feathers.
35 – 39%	Generally weak in its ability to convey black; poor, limited or incoherent.	Barbeque briquettes, Guinness Original, the photocopy of a photocopy, videotape, shading with the flat of an HB pencil.
20 – 34%	Insufficiently black; black reproduced in a disjointed or decontextualised manner; fails to draw on important sources of black.	Classroom blackboards, Pomfret cakes, cavolo nero, thermal till roll lettering, pizza olives.
0- 19%	Negligent in its handling of black.	The photocopy of a photocopy of a photocopy, magnetic cassette tape, bin liners, shading with the flat of a 9H pencil, schoolyard tarmac during a short drought.

SONNET

Monday a.m.
Monday p.m.

Tuesday a.m.
Tuesday p.m.

Wednesday a.m.
Wednesday p.m.

Thursday a.m.
Thursday p.m.

Friday a.m.
Friday p.m.

Saturday a.m.
Saturday p.m.

Sunday a.m.
Sunday p.m.

BIRTHDAY POEM FOR RODDY LUMSDEN

If I think of ping-pong balls I think of rusty scissors. If I think
of shadows I think of cold baked beans. If I think of aspirin
I think of walking uphill. If I think of walking uphill I think
of jam.

If I think of record shops or tins of red paint I think of the
difficulties I have in making plans with my friends. If I think
of vocabulary I think of mousetraps. If I think of footprints I
think of wasps.

If I think of brickwork I think of hard soap. If I think of
sparrows I think of string. If I think of Roddy Lumsden I
think of Roddy Lumsden in a creaky chair, singing in a
whisper in the dark.

*

If I think of coffee cups I think of the gap in the railings. If
I think of the breadboard I think of walking alone. If I think
of coathanger wire or reef knots I think of the tangibility of
thought.

If I think of lucozade I think of dandelions. I think of letraset.
I think of the gap in my teeth. If I think about handwriting
I'll wonder if place isn't simply the routes we've taken to get
here.

If I think of doughnuts I think of sawdust. If I think of
mittens I think of mud. If I think of Roddy Lumsden I think
of Roddy Lumsden polishing an apple on the sleeve of his
green corduroy shirt.

*

I think of yo-yos. I think of coconuts. I think of buying peanut butter in bulk. If I think of tarmac I think of stamps. I think of walking home through the woods in the rain.

If I think about noodles I think of double rainbows and whether a new experience is an excuse to do what we always do. If I think of light bulbs I think of group photos. If I think of group photos I think of faded jeans.

If I think of vinegar I think of the gaps in my vocabulary. If I think of my penknife I think of the estuary at low tide. If I think of Roddy Lumsden I think of Roddy Lumsden at the window, the strip lights casting his shadow out across the yard.

3 PIECES WITH SEMI-COLONS

in summer, a lemon; in autumn, a lemon; in winter and spring, nothing other than a lemon.

the effect of the temperature in the room on the lemons; the effect of the lemons on the temperature in the room.

the idea of a lemon, the idea of a firm lemon, a firm idea of a lemon; the idea of a lemon, the idea of a loose lemon, a loose idea of a lemon.

POEM IN WHICH I RIFF ON THE PULP SONG 'DISHES' IN WHICH THE LINE 'I AM NOT JESUS THOUGH I HAVE THE SAME INITIALS' IS SUNG BY JARVIS COCKER

I am not Muddy Waters, though I have the same initials.
I am not Marina Warner, though I have the same initials.
I am not Mae West or the Mid West, though I have the same initials.

I am not Mary Wesley. I am not a 'My Waitrose' card.
I am not Anna May Wong, though I have some of the same initials.

I am not Mike Watt and I am not Max Wall.
I am not a magic wand and I am not a mealworm.

I am not Mary Whitehouse or Michelle Williams.
I am not Meg White, Murray Walker or the Mugwumps.

I am not Mal Waldron. I am not Mark Waldron.
I am not a Mexican wave, the March winds, a miracle worker, mulled
    wine, or mucky wellingtons.

I am not Warren Mitchell, though I have an inversion of the same
    initials.
I am not Wes Morgan or Wendy Mulford or William Morris.

I am not the Merriam-Webster dictionary.
I am not Medium Wave radio.

I am not the Frank Sinatra song 'My Way', though I have the same
    initials.

I am not Mohammed Walait, though I am his next-door neighbour and we do have the same initials.

I am not the Milky Way.
I am not a Milky Way.

I am not malt whisky, Mighty White bread, or malted wheatflakes.
I am not a makeweight. I am not a middleweight.

I am not Marion Welton, though she is, indeed, my mother and, indeed, we do have the same initials.

A BIRD GUIDE TO NOTTINGHAM

Robin

Goose

Magpies

Duck

POEM IN WHICH THE TWENTY WORDS MOST COMMON IN HEAVY METAL LYRICS ARE USED

for Alex MacDonald

Though we're aware there are moments when the form sorrow takes will mean a reduction in our awareness of things, it is in those moments that our awareness perhaps becomes insufficient for us to counteract the effect our sorrow will have on how aware we are. My sleepy demon tells me he doesn't mind stumping up for the pizzas, but insists we're gonna go halves on the beer. The television plays quietly; the candles on my cake burn low.

It's been a wet afternoon so my sleepy demon suggests a game of scream-like-you-mean-it and though, after the visit from the police has made me feel I could reasonably claim victory, my sleepy demon keeps at it until the budgie is breathing audibly, and the air smells like rusty cutlery, and the tv channels are flipping between a difficult quiz show and championship ping-pong. I get a hunch there's something gunky in his veins. There's a box of tissues in the kitchen, but when he cries he doesn't use them. I've a hunch there's something silty in his soul. Between us we've practically completed the crossword.

My sleepy demon shows me a photo of a bunch of younger demons, leaning against a wooden door in their baggy yellow sweaters. He smokes, and taps the ashes into a lemonade can. The more he stares at the candle flames, the more they appear to splutter. The notes that I told my therapist were an account of my dreams are, in reality, just some paragraphs I copied from a sci-fi novel.

My sleepy demon hands me a page from a spiral-bound notebook on which he has written 'a mood of resignation reigns'. The takeaway menus and till receipts are already in shreds, but now we tear up our coffee-shop loyalty cards, the tv-licence renewal notice, a club-night flyer, a jiffy bag, the amaretti wrappers, the street map, some pages from his notebook and my hospital appointment letter. Sometimes when I'm queuing for coffee or picking up the phone or getting onto a train, I like to pray there's somebody somewhere getting all this on camera.

My sleepy demon reckons I'm confusing the idea of eternity with the idea of the passage of time, and while, he says, what I'm anticipating is the continuing rotation of winters/summers, morning/evening, weekdays/weekends, what I've got coming is an unbudging moment sometime early in March where across the town the drizzle is consistently thickening and in the kitchen the strip lights seem particularly yellow. A small sleepy beast crawls in through the cat flap, and my sleepy demon offers it the pizza crusts and the complimentary tub of hummus.

In the goodbye note he pins to my door, my sleepy demon expresses an ethical objection to metaphor. There are, he hints, particular gods whose brief it is to make things easy for us so that when the gods whose brief is to test our resolve get on the case the test will be sterner and the results will give a truer picture. In the evening I'll sit in the kitchen with my yo-yo and a new box of ping-pong balls, and I'll barely even have to breathe before the candles blow out.

POEM FOR LEAH WILKINS

the
dumper

truck
drivers

fry
pumpkins

for
supper

EIGHT PIECES
IN IMITATION OF THOMAS A. CLARK

an infinite future
of hatchlings, buds, saplings –
the footpaths, mulch, pebbles
of the infinite past

=

the coherence of cloud
the fluency of wind
the articulation
of a chaffinch's song

=

the movements of still things –
streams, soil, ferns in the breeze;
the stillness of moving things –
falling leaves, clouds, hours

=

where the slope of the hill
grows suddenly gradual –
where the slope of the hill
grows suddenly acute

=

the green leaves on the branch
the dead leaves on the ground
the dead leaves on the branch
the green leaves on the ground

=

vertical trees along
horizontal footpaths –
their trunks in the sunlight
their trunks in the shadow

=

what it is about the stream
that the earth won't absorb it –
what it is about the earth
that it won't absorb the stream

=

the aptness of the air
to the buzzing of flies –
the aptness of the flies
to the buzzing of air

AWESOME
for Amelia MacDonald

Awesome! says the albatross

Bother! says the bullfinch

Claptrap! says the cockatoo

Drat! says the drake

Eek! says the emu

Fiddlesticks! says the falcon

Guff! says the goose

Hokum! says the hawk

Impossible! says the ibis

Jeepers! says the jay

Ka-pow! says the kiwi

Lumme! says the linnet

Mamma mia! says the magpie

Nuts! says the nightingale

Oops! says the ostrich

Quack! says the quail

Ridiculous! says the robin

Shucks! says the shrike

Tut-tut! says the toucan

Ugh! says the umbrellabird

Vile! says the vulture

Whatever! says the whippoorwill

XXXX! says the xema

Yikes! says the yellowhammer

Zut! says the zebra finch

The jittery twin sends us a mix tape of tunes for six-fingered pianists. The wheezy twin unzips her zebra suit. As we cycle by the magnet factory, the weepy twin's bicycle wobbles.

The rain holds off while the snarly twin dismantles the tent and reloads the trailer. The freckly twin gives us a ride in the watermelon truck. The sweaty twin's pockets bulge with ping-pong balls.

The tin of pickled sticklebacks rusts in the shivery twin's cupboard. The wordy twin's key snaps off in the lock. We spend an evening removing the darts from the queasy twin's photo.

The drowsy twin digs up our radishes. The zesty twin breaks the silence by reciting times tables. The hazelnuts drops through the hole in the mouthy twin's pocket.

The giggly twin sneaks in through the unlatched skylight. The woozy twin takes a bite from each apple in the basket. We dawdle on the footbridge until the lanky twin has cycled by, twice.

POEM

a lemon in
the pocket

of her denim
dungarees –

an envelope
of lemon seeds

in the pocket
of her shirt

You are not George Best, the footballer, though George Best shares your birthday. And you are not Katie Price, the model and author, though Katie Price also shares your birthday.

You are not the Wars of the Roses, though the Wars of the Roses began on the date of your birthday in 1455. And you are not Dustin Moskovitz, the co-founder of Facebook, though you and Dustin Moskovitz share a birthday.

You are not the singer Morrissey though Morrissey shares your birthday. You are not the Lewis and Clark Expedition, though the Lewis and Clark Expedition began on the date of your birthday, departing from St. Charles, Missouri in 1804.

Though the riots in Littleport, Cambridgeshire, which took place over high unemployment and rising grain costs, took place on the date of your birthday in 1816, you are not the Littleport riots.

Though you share a birthday with him, you are not the politician Menzies Campbell. And you are not the abolition in 1840 of the transportation of British convicts to the penal colony of New South Wales.

You are not the patent issued to Abraham Lincoln for an invention for lifting boats, which was issued on the date of your birthday in 1849, or the patent for the Flying-Machine, which was issued to Orville and Wilbur Wright on the date of your birthday in 1906.

You are not Langston Hughes, the poet, though the anniversary of his death takes place on your birthday. You are not the collision of three trains in Quintinshill near Gretna Green on the date of your birthday in 1915.

You are not the International Day for Biological Diversity, though the International Day for Biological Diversity is now held on your birthday. You are not Naomi Campbell, the model and author, though Naomi Campbell shares your birthday.

You are not the capture of Fallujah by British troops in 1941 or the disbandment of the Commintern in 1943 or the South African government's approval in 1957 of racial separation in universities.

Though he shares your birthday, you are not the lyricist Bernie Taupin. And though his death occurred on the date of your birthday, you are not the former poet laureate, Cecil Day-Lewis.

You are not Lyndon B. Johnson's introduction in 1958 of the Great Society and you are not Richard Nixon's confession in 1973 to his role in the Watergate affair. You are not World Goth Day.

You are not the Smiths' single 'Bigmouth Strikes Again', which was released on the date of your birthday in 1986, and you are not the 2015 Irish referendum on the legalization of gay marriage. You are not the tennis player Novak Djokovic though, as you are celebrating your birthday, Novak Djokovic will be celebrating his.

A BIRD GUIDE TO PLYMOUTH

for Anthony Caleshu

Drake

POEM IN A SINGLE BREATH

for Kathryn Williams

You've been singing along with the radio all morning
and I sit here turning pages without really reading

and your fingers smell like vinegar
and we think we hear the doorbell

and, as the shadows sharpen and you prop
open the window, the drizzle seems to ease.

We think it's our thoughts that are distorting how we see things,
though we wonder if it's what we see that is distorting our thoughts.

The sunlight catches the spider-webs
and I can't really hear what you're saying

and somebody's used up the peanut butter
as we'd imagined somebody might.

FIVE PIECES, EACH OF 250 WORDS

#1

On Big Bill Broonzy's *Trouble in Mind* album there are nineteen songs, of which twelve were recorded around March 1957 at the Dancing Slipper club on Central Avenue in West Bridgford at a concert organised by a one-armed jazz promoter whose nickname was Lefty.

Although I didn't know the titles of any of his albums, I'd heard a couple of tapes by Big Bill Broonzy, and when I filled in a *wants* card at Good Vibrations on Mansfield Road I just listed the names of all the songs of his that I had come across.

The book *Big Bill Blues* features an account of how a black woman, who'd imagined it would be easier to find work in Chicago than in the South, queues all day in an employment office only for her number never to get called, to which Broonzy comments 'it's the same soup, but it's just served in a different way.'

The footage in which Big Bill Broonzy sits in the sun on the porch of a wooden house and strums 'Stump Blues' and 'Hey, hey' was made the day before he underwent his operation for throat cancer, in July 1957, and was shot by Pete Seeger on a 16mm Auricon camera.

As I write this the sky is already a deep smudgy blue and though the days are still warm and it'll be weeks before we even begin thinking about college, something of the hush of autumn is nudging its way into my understanding of things.

2

While it is broadly understood that Pete Seeger's response to Bob Dylan's use of an electric guitar and an amplified backing band at the 1965 Newport Folk Festival was to take an axe to the electrical cables, it has been suggested that this is a misunderstanding which grew out of a comment made onstage by the festival announcer during the moments of cheering and booing following the three-song set of electric blues.

At least some of the people in the audience were calling for Dylan to return to the stage with an acoustic guitar, and while in the announcer's use of the phrase 'he's gonna get his axe', 'he' has usually been taken to refer to Seeger and 'axe' has usually been understood in literal terms, the possibility that the pronoun was in fact being used to refer to Dylan and 'axe' was being used as hipster slang for guitar puts things into a different perspective.

The fact that earlier that July day Pete Seeger had given a performance of a traditional work song in which he had kept time by chopping wood with an authentic lumberjack's axe may be an element in the way this matter has been perceived.

My copy of the live album of Pete Seeger's 1963 concert at Carnegie Hall was among the many Pete Seeger records in the second-hand racks at Good Vibrations.

As I write this there are crows on the greenhouse roof and the snow on the windowsills is already beginning to thaw.

3

Of the ten songs on Bob Dylan's *Modern Times* album, four use the structure of the twelve-bar blues.

The sixteen verses of 'The Levee's Gonna Break' are bunched into fours, with a guitar solo after each bunch. The repetition of the title phrase constitutes a defining element of the song's structure. In two of the verses the phrase 'some of these people' is sung in the concluding line; in two of the others the phrase 'some people' is used.

In 'Someday Baby' the first two lines of each verse comprise a rhyme. The unrhymed third line is identical in all nine verses.

The words of 'Thunder on the Mountain' fit into quatrains with an aabb rhyme scheme. One couplet is sung over the first four bars and the second is stretched across the next eight. The twelve verses of the song are bunched into threes, and each bunch is rounded off with a guitar break. The title phrase is sung in the first line of the first verse in each bunch.

'The Levee's Gonna Break' and 'Rolling and Tumbling' are both blues of the kind in which the second line is a restatement of the first.

At the time of the record's release *The Observer* published an interview Bob Dylan gave to Jonathan Lethem.

I downloaded the record track-by-track from Limewire, though when my misgivings got the better of me I bought it for a fiver from Fopp.

As I write this there are blackbirds gathering twigs in my yard.

#4

In its examination of what the idea of creativity might involve, Jonathan Lethem's essay 'The Ecstasy of Influence' discusses how the description Muddy Waters gives of the way he wrote his song 'Country Blues' includes a number of possibly contradictory accounts, including being taught it by another guitar player, it coming from the cotton field, and, as he was fixing a puncture and feeling blue about a girl, the song falling into his mind.

While the first Jonathan Lethem book I read was *The Fortress of Solitude*, which at the time I bought it had been published four years, and the second was *Motherless Brooklyn*, which had been published eight years, the first I was able to respond to as something entirely new – I remember reading a review in *The Guardian* and seeing copies of it piled on the *recent releases* table in the Arndale Centre branch of Waterstone's – was *You Don't Love Me Yet*, which came out in 2007.

As I write this it feels like nothing can disturb the stuffy summery heat, and the imprecision that's getting into everything is meaning the bed linen is feeling scratchy and the radio is playing louder and the flies in the kitchen have it in mind that by circulating beneath the strip lights in a loosely triangular formation they'll somehow come to terms with the principles on which things interact, and then the drizzle will drag in through the city again and our voices will become unresonant and tuneless and raspy.

5

In the footage of his 1977 concert at the Molde Jazz Festival, the audience doesn't applaud the piano solo in 'Prison Bound Blues' until Muddy Waters explicitly prompts them to.

The volume switches on Muddy Waters's Telecaster were the *chickenhead* switches he had removed from his amplifier.

Unless I play it at maximum volume, the album of Big Bill Broonzy songs recorded by Muddy Waters in 1960, which I downloaded from i-Tunes, can be particularly difficult to listen to.

Muddy Waters began using an electric guitar and playing with an amplified backing band when he moved to Chicago from Mississippi in 1943.

The performance that a number of American blues singers gave in the rain at Wilbraham Road station was broadcast by Granada TV in 1964.

There's an extended passage in the footage of Muddy Waters's 1960 Newport Jazz Festival performance which features close-ups of the feet of audience members twitching in time to the music.

When Fender produced its Artist Series Muddy Waters Telecaster, it came with the amplifier switches already fitted.

I bought the DVD of the performances at the jazz festivals at Newport, Copenhagen and Molde from the Rough Trade shop in Portobello Road.

During the encore at the Newport concert Muddy Waters dances ballroom-style with his harmonica player.

As I write this there's a dripping tap keeping time with the recording of 'You're gonna miss me when I'm dead and gone' and the breeze from the kitchen window is ruffling the pencil-sharpenings piled on my desk.

POEM FOR LAURIE CLARK

nine

ten

a lemon

twelve

ACKNOWLEDGMENTS

It would not be possible to imagine this book without the friendship, support and influence of Thomas A. Clark and Laurie Clark. It was Tom and Laurie's Moschatel Press that published the original sixteen-section *Squid Squad* book in 2017, from which the version presented here developed. Tom and Laurie's Cairn Gallery produced a poster edition of the poem '3 pieces with semi-colons'. Along with the two poems whose titles bear their names, the other pieces to have grown most directly out of Tom and Laurie Clark's input are 'Green Gauge', 'Blues Scale' and 'Black List'. I owe them both my deepest thanks.

Further sections of *Squid Squad* have been published in *Cordite Poetry Review*, *Shuddhashar*, *The Times Literary Supplement*, *The Manchester Review*. My thanks to the editors Holly Isemonger, Ahmedur Rashid Chowdhury, Alan Jenkins, John McAuliffe and Chad Campbell.

'Which of us is it I am?': commissioned for *The Caught Habits of Language, An Entertainment for W.S. Graham for Him Having Reached One Hundred*, edited by Rachael Boast, Andy Ching and Nathan Hamilton, published by Donut Press.

'Poem for Sarah Jackson': a recording of the poem was included in the Dial-a-Poem project, curated by Sarah Jackson.

'Green Gauge', 'Blues Scale', 'Black List': first published in *para-text* issue 3, edited by Laura Elliott and Angus Sinclair.

'Birthday Poem for Roddy Lumsden': included in the private publication Poems for Roddy, edited by Lavinia Singer.

'Poem in which I riff on the Pulp song "Dishes" in which the line "I am not Jesus though I have the same initials" is sung by Jarvis Cocker': published in *The Other Room Anthology 10*, edited by James Davies, Scott Thurston and Tom Jenks.

'A bird guide to Nottingham': produced as a poster and postcard for the Words for Walls project, edited by Nicola Thomas and Philip Jones.

'Poem in which the twenty words most common in heavy metal lyrics are used': published in *Poems in which 10*, edited by Rebecca Perry, Alex MacDonald, Amy Key and Wayne Holloway-Smith.

'Poem in Yr Pocket': produced as a card by Five Leaves Bookshop, edited by Leah Wilkins.

'Eight Pieces in Imitation of Thomas A. Clark': published in *Granta* 134 by poetry editor Rachael Allen.

'Poem ('a lemon in')': featured in the exhibition *Paint Her to Your Own Mind* at Shandy Hall, Coxwold, curated by Patrick Wildgust.

'Poem in a single breath', commissioned by Kathryn Williams for her Coming Up For Air project of performances and recordings.

'Five Pieces, each of 250 words': published as a pamphlet by If a Leaf Falls press, edited by Sam Riviere.

Thank you to the editors and curators of all these projects and publications.

Thanks are also due to Sam Buchan-Watts, Sue Dymoke, Gary Snapper, Richard Skinner, Larry Goves, John McAuliffe, Jon McGregor, Lynda Pratt and Michael Schmidt.